"It's Not Fair!"

Knowing What's Right, What's Not, and What You Can Do About It

Written by
Linus Mundy

Illustrated by
R. W. Alley

ONE
CARING
PLACE

Abbey Press
St. Meinrad, IN 47577

Dedicated to
Graham Richard Wolkenberg...
May you live happily in a world that is more fair
and more just with each passing year.

Text © 2014 Linus Mundy
Illustrations © 2014 Saint Meinrad Archabbey
Published by One Caring Place
Abbey Press
St. Meinrad, Indiana 47577

Library of Congress Catalog Number
2013922755

ISBN 978-0-87029-560-7

Printed in the United States of America

A Message to Parents, Teachers, and Other Caring Adults

When it comes to fairness, every kid knows that a parent can't break a candy bar perfectly in half for sharing. We grown-ups also know what it's like not being treated fairly; but we have had experience and time to try to figure out just why our world is not totally fair. We know, for example, that unfairness springs from such things as greed, hatred, anger, prejudice, misunderstanding, or even from the ways of Nature.

But using these "big words" to explain unfairness to children will probably not work. And so in this book, we try to use smaller words and examples that children will understand and relate to. The colorful, marvelous illustrations by R.W. Alley will surely help make this book a happy learning experience.

In his or her innocence, your child's world would be one of perfect equality and fairness. And from the viewpoint of us parents, teachers, and other caring adults, we would make it this kind of world if we only could—a world where kids and adults were safer, where the world's goods were shared fairly, where all children (and all adults, too, for that matter) were given equal access to healthcare, education, a loving home, a government with laws and policies made for the benefit of all. Fairness, one must understand, is not always about giving everyone the same thing, either. More often it is about providing people with what they need. So, for example, some students may be allowed more time than others for a test because they need more time. That is not unfair.

This book, then, is written in an effort to help you and your child make the world better, but also to teach the child that his or her world is bigger and broader and wider still than they sometimes think or feel or experience. Our children are ready to understand more about this big, wide world we live in. And they are, like you, ready to make it better for everyone, by making it more just, more fair.

—Linus Mundy

Being Treated Fairly

Isn't it nice when you work hard on something at school—and then you end up getting a good grade and your teacher says, "Good job"?

Or you help your dad wash the car and the car is really dirty and you work hard and get water all over yourself, too, but you don't care because your dad says, "It is so nice to have your help."

Or maybe your mom asks you to watch over your little brother while she steps outside to pick up the mail or the newspaper. You say, "Sure, Mom!" and your little brother comes running to you and gives you a big hug.

Sometimes Things Don't Seem Fair

Imagine you worked very hard on a painting for art class and you think it looks really good. But your teacher says, "You can do better than this. The colors are all wrong." Maybe she's right, but it might not seem fair.

Or maybe you helped your mom make dinner and, even though you tried to be careful, you still made a mess and your mom got upset. That doesn't seem fair.

Sometimes, no matter how hard we try, things might not go our way... and that doesn't seem fair.

Some Things Aren't So Bad

Imagine you wanted to act in the school play, but didn't get a part. That might feel unfair. But, maybe you discover that you have a real talent in helping design the scenes or costumes for the actors to wear.

Or, what if it poured down rain on the day of your ballgame? Even though your day might seem ruined, it turned out OK, because you get to go to a friend's house and play with her.

Sometimes things that seem unfair, turn out to be not so bad.

So Much Unfairness That IS Bad

Have you ever watched the news and seen pictures of people whose houses were all blown down by a tornado? Maybe some of the people were even injured or died.

Sometimes we hear about a terrible accident and wonder why bad things happen.

There are things in the world that are not fair, and we can't always understand them.

Some Things Are Unfair and We Can't Do Anything About Them

There are times when things happen that don't seem fair, but we simply can't do anything about them.

Imagine you're at home sick in bed on the very day that your class goes on a field trip to the zoo. It doesn't seem fair that you can't be there eating ice cream with your friends and watching the monkeys play.

Some Things Are Unfair but We CAN Do Something About Them

What if your friend got injured in a bicycle accident and couldn't go outside to play? You could ask your mom or dad to take you to his house for a little while, so you can help cheer him up.

Maybe the animal shelter in your neighborhood is full of cats and dogs that need a home. You could talk to your parents about adopting one or spend time visiting the animals.

Sometimes even just talking about your feelings when things seem unfair is a way to make things better.

You Can Help Make the World More Fair

There are little things and big things we can do to make the world more fair for people everywhere.

Maybe you can be part of a group at school that raises money for fighting cancer or helps a hospital for children. Or, you can tell your mom and dad it's OK to use some of the Christmas money this year for a family without much money. You will still get presents, but so will people you don't even know!

Someday, when you grow up, you could become a firefighter, a nurse, a minister, or teacher and really help people with what they need.

Sharing Is One Great Way to Make Life More Fair

If your friend always has the same yucky sandwich at lunchtime, give him half of your cool peanut butter and jelly sandwich.

Inviting a friend to play with your newest video game, or ride your new bike is also a nice thing to do.

It isn't fair for someone to stand out in the rain without an umbrella. So, share yours when you have one to share.

Sports and Playtime Can Seem Very Unfair

If Joey is always the last one picked for a team because he strikes out a lot, it would make him feel awfully happy if someone chose him early, even one time.

The bigger kids always take over the playground and tell you to go away. You know it's not fair. Maybe you can ask your teacher about big and little kids taking turns.

If Sabrina is always the one who takes over the soccer ball and takes all the shots, maybe you and some other kids can ask her—in a nice way—to share more.

It Feels Like Grown-Ups Get to Do Everything!

Maybe you waited all winter to go to the amusement park and try out the new ride everyone told you about. But it turns out you are too short to ride and you have to wait till next year!

Try to remember that you, too, will be older and bigger someday and you will get your turn.

Also, try to remember that older kids and grown-ups have more things to worry about and take care of. And even big kids and grown-ups don't get to do everything they want!

You Can Speak Up When Things Seem Unfair

If your mom is angry at you for not cleaning your room—and you just did clean your room—you might need to show her. Maybe your dad promised to read you a book at bedtime, but he forgot. It's OK to remind him that he made a promise. After all, moms and dads can make mistakes, too.

If you notice that something is wrong and nobody else notices, speak up! It's OK to try to make things fair.

Life Is Not All Good and Life Is Not All Bad

Sometimes we are lucky. We get things we may not even deserve. And, sometimes, when unfair things happen, good things can still happen in the end.

A forest fire may destroy miles and miles of trees. But before you know it, new little trees are sprouting up everywhere in the ashes!

Your mom comes home from the hospital with a new baby. Even though you worry that you will have to share everything with him, it turns out that you really like having a little brother.

Sometimes We Wonder Why God Doesn't FIX Things That Are Unfair

You may see a person on the sidewalk with a sign that says: "Lost my job. I am hungry." You might see people give him some money. That is God working through others.

People are hurt in car accidents every day. The injured people are rushed to the hospital, and the doctors and nurses make them well again and the car is fixed at a car repair shop.

We may wonder why God isn't there to help. But God is there—in the good people at the hospital, in the ambulance, and even in the repair shop where they fix the car.

We Make Our World More Fair Together

When we see something wrong, we can usually do something—at least a little bit—to make things better.

Sometimes it takes only one person—just you or me—to do or say something and…Presto! things can be better and more fair.

But mostly it takes all of us, big kids and little kids, moms and dads, cousins and neighbors, strangers and friends, all over the world to make a real difference. And that's very fair—all of us doing our part!

Linus Mundy has written several other books in the "Elf-help" and "Elf-help Books for Kids" series, including *Slow-down Therapy* for grown-ups, and *When Bad Things Happen,* for children. His wife, Michaelene, has written many children's books, including the "Elf-help Books for Kids," *Sad Isn't Bad,* and *Mad Isn't Bad*. The Mundys live in southern Indiana, and have recently been blessed with their first grandchild, Graham.

R. W. Alley is the illustrator for the popular Abbey Press series of Elf-help books, as well as an illustrator and writer of children's books. He lives in Barrington, Rhode Island, with his wife, daughter, and son. See a wide variety of his works at: www.rwalley.com.